A. Goring Thomas, Frederick Corder, B. C. Stephenson

The Golden Web

Comedy Opera in Three Acts

A. Goring Thomas, Frederick Corder, B. C. Stephenson

The Golden Web
Comedy Opera in Three Acts

ISBN/EAN: 9783337126681

Printed in Europe, USA, Canada, Australia, Japan

Cover: Foto ©Andreas Hilbeck / pixelio.de

More available books at **www.hansebooks.com**

THE GOLDEN WEB

Comedy Opera

IN THREE ACTS
by

F. CORDER AND B.C. STEPHENSON

Lyrics by F. Corder

MUSIC BY

ARTHUR GORING THOMAS.

London,
CHAPPELL & C.º 50. NEW BOND STREET. W.
NEW YORK · NOVELLO · EWER & C.º

Written for and produced by the **Carl Rosa Light Opera Company**, at the Royal Court Theatre, Liverpool. on Wednesday, Feb.15th, 1893.

DRAMATIS PERSONÆ.

LORD SILVERTOP . . . . . *Bass* . . . . An old Beau.

BULLION . . . . *Bass* . . . . A rich London Merchant.

GEOFFREY NORREYS . . . *Tenor* . . . . A young Spendthrift.

DR. MANACLE . . . . *Baritone* . . . . . A Fleet Parson.

SPINDLE . . . . *Bass* . . . . His man.

SMUG . . . . *Bass* . . . . Lord Silvertop's Valet.

AMABEL . . . . *Soprano* . . . . . Bullion's Niece.

MISTRESS PAMELA PATCH . . *Contralto* . . . . . . Her Aunt.

MRS. SCATTERWELL . . . . *Soprano* ⎫
⎬ . . . . . Ladies of Fashion.
MRS. POUNCEBY . . . . . . *Contralto* ⎭

Bailiffs, Touts, Citizens, Ladies & Gentlemen, &c

ACT I.—The Fleet Market.   ACT II.—Ranelagh Gardens.

ACT III.—Interior of The Golden Web.

PERIOD 1750.

Contents.

THE GOLDEN WEB.

OVERTURE.

18796.

4

18796.

18796.

18796.

18796.

12

18796,

ACT I.

CHORUS WITH SOLOS (SPINDLE AND MANACLE.)

Noise and tu_mult, noise and tu_mult ev_'ry_where!

Noise and tu_mult, noise and tu_mult ev_'ry_where! Nought ro_

Noise and tu_mult, noise and tu_mult ev_'ry_where!

Noise and tu_mult, noise and tu_mult ev_'ry_where! Nought ro_

Nought ro_man_tic, All men fran_tic, Seek_ing gold with

_man_tic, All men fran_tic, Seek_ing gold with

Nought ro_man_tic, All men fran_tic, Seek_ing

_man_tic, All men fran_tic, Seek_ing gold with

(TOUTS.)
1ST GROUP

1. Sweet couple be ad — vis'd, Be ad — vis'd, and

1. step........ this way,.. 2ND GROUP.

2. Nay here's the shop where there is least to

1. Be ad — vis'd,........ and step this way.

3RD GROUP.

2. pay. Fair madam, marry

18796.

We give a proper stamp'd cer_ti_fi_cate.

we at on_ly half the rate,

And so do we at on_ly half.... the rate.

cres.

And so do we at on_ly

cres.

Fair madam, mar ry here.

half the rate, at on_ly half. the rate.

So step this way.

cres.

cres.

f

SPINDLE. *Andante*

Fleet par-sons weddings Cannot be maintain'd. My master

has been properly or - dain'd. *Tempo I^{mo}.*

A - way! They're mine, I

A - way! They're mine, I

A way! They're mine, I

Nay, nay!

WOMEN.

Oh pray! oh pray your con - flict stay!

MEN.

Your con - flict

say! Who dares my stur - dy arm gain say?

say! Who

fran _ tic Seeking gold with strife gi _ gan tic, _ 'Tis their on _ ly

Seeking gold with strife gi _ gan _ _ tic, with strife gi _

All men fran _ tic, Seek _ ing gold with strife,....... with strife gi _

Seeking gold with strife gi _ gan _ _ tic, with strife gi _

care........... Beaux so wit _ ty, Maids so pret _ ty, Ah

_ gan _ _ tic... Beaux so wit _ ty, Maids so pret _ ty, Ah what a

_ gan _ _ tic. Beaux so wit _ ty, Maids so pret _ ty, Ah what a

_ gan _ _ tic. Beaux so wit _ ty, Maids so pret _ ty, Ah

18796.

'Tis a serious matter when love..... flies a _ bout, Dis-

charg _ ing his arrows at ran _ dom. Not even the old _ est.... his power can

scout, Nor mere children who scarce under.stand.... them.

'Tis a serious mat _ ter when love flies a_

sought... but a loose knot the ... I tell you... no pow'r can un_

_bind you, Think not that the Church.... you can lightly de_fy,... Or stern,....

retribution will find you!.. Think not... that the

Church you can lightly de_fy or stern retribution will find .... you, And when on the

cres.

cres.

f

p

colla voce.

M.
... the most serious mat _ ter of all!

_ ter of all!

_ r of all!

TEN: *Moderato.*
A _ ha! That was a sermon un ex _ pect _ ed! See how they slink away with

BASS:
A _ ha! That was a sermon un ex _ pect _ ed! See how they slink away with

mien de _ ject _ ed! Fare _ well! Fare _ well!

mien de _ ject _ ed! Fare _ well! Fare _

Seek _ ing gold with strife gi _ gan _ tic,___ 'Tis their on _ ly care,.....

Seek _ ing gold with strife gi _ gan _ _ tic, with strife gi _ gan _ tic.

fran _ tic, Seek _ ing gold with strife,...... with strife gi _ gan _ tic.

Seek _ ing gold with strife gi _ gan _ _ tic, with strife gi _ gan _ tic.

.... their on _ ly care,. Oh what a place is London

Yes, 'tis their on _ ly care......

Oh what a place is London ci _ _ ty,

Yes, 'tis their on _ ly care...... Yes,

cres:

CHORUS, WITH RECIT. (GEOFFREY.)

He speaks the truth.   Come,.... let him go!

He speaks the

Yes,   yes,   let him

truth....   Come,....   let him go,   yes,   let him

go!   Thou hast de_fraud_ed us!

go!   Thou hast de_fraud_ed us!

♩=♩. of preceding movement.

f

Recit: **GEOFFREY** (throwing them off.)

Thus do I treat whoever dares to call me cheat!

Allegro.

Poco Andante.

Fine friends are ye who hang on me and win my gold! Un_til I

stand a wreck complete! Then, greedy for more spoil, ye raise this

Allegro.

TEN:

BASS.

din. Well! pay thy debts!

Well!.... pay' thy debts!

GEOFF: *Recit:*

I have lost

Recit:

Moderato.

nay, good friend, be not so rash!..... We'll wait un_til you've

Nay, good friend be not so rash!... We'll

got more cash!..... Put up your sword,... we're not a_fraid!

wait un_til you've got more cash! we're not a_fraid!

But we had rather not be paid!.. Nay, nay,

But we had rather not be paid!.. Good

Be not so rash!....

friend, be not so rash!

Put up your

we're not afraid! But we had rather not.... be

sword, we're not afraid! But we had rather not.... be

colla voce.

Allegro.

paid!...

paid!...

Allegro.

No. 3.

RECIT: & SONG (GEOFFREY)

GEOFF: *Recit.*

The cowards! how they take to heel At the first

sight of honest steel! Fool! Fool!

Allegro.

Recit. *Moderato.*

... to seek a mid such scenes .... as these Dis _

_ trac _ tion for a heart bereft of ease! ....

18796.

G. loves...... de _ cay...... Sum _ mer, thy leaves turn'd to

G. gold.... 'ere they pe _ rished. The gold I cherish'd turns to

G. wi _ _ ther'd leaves! A _ las!.... a _ las!.... that the

G. world and its treasures Our loves and plea _ sures a _ like......

trea _ sures Our loves . . . . and

plea _ sures a _ like . . . . . must pass,

must pass, ... must . . .

pass! . . . .

a tempo.

18796.

No.4.

TRIO (GEOFFREY, MANACLE AND SPINDLE.)

Manacle.
Wilt thou take whom_e'er I bring,
Countess, cook, or a_ny thing, Mar_ry her..... for
good, or ill?..... Then the man shall say. "I

Spindle.

Geoff:
Will she take.... me
will, I will!"

18796

18796.

18796.

S. _ sue, The plan to gether well pur_ sue!.. Come

marriage bell... Altho' we do not know What kind of she The bride will be,

bell, Altho' we do not know What kind of she The bride will be, And..

ring the merry bell, Al_tho' we do not know The kind of she The bride will be,

May blessings on her flow, And bless_ ings on the happy pair.... who part as

... may blessings on her flow, And bless_ ings on the hap_ py pair.... who

May blessings on her flow,.... And blessings on the hap_ py

18796.

18796.

SCENA (AMABEL.)

souls, to-ge-ther feel-ing strong.

Allegro.

cres - _cen -_ _do._

Oh

dear, I am so frighten'd, My pulse is mad-ly

heigh _-ten'd,_ And ev' _-ry_ nerve is tight _-en'd._ Aunt

cres:

Pa _ me _ la, Aunt Pa _ me _ la is lost!

Oh dear,....... I am so

frighten'd!

Aunt Pa _

_ me _ la is lost, A _ las,..... is

lost!............ I turn'd my head a

18796.

No. 6. QUINTET (Amabel, Pamela, Geoffrey, Manacle & Spindle.)

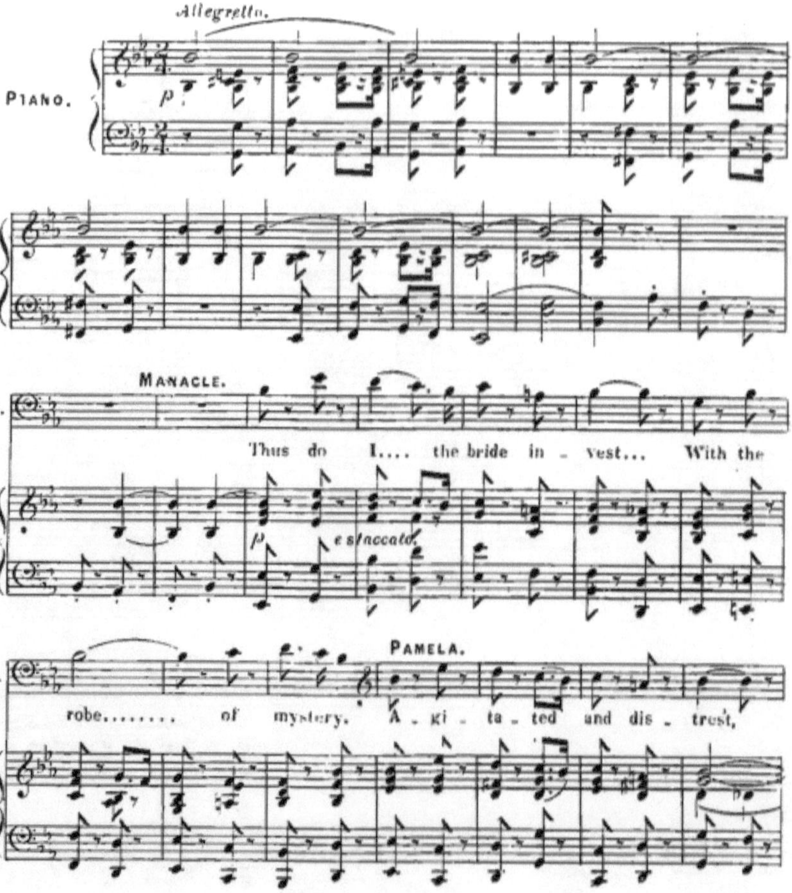
Allegretto.
Piano.
p
Manacle.
M.
Thus do I.... the bride in - vest... With the
p
e staccato.
M.
robe........ of mystery.
Pamela.
A - gi - ta - ted and dis - trest,
P.
Dark - - er trou - bles I.... for - see.
Spindle.
Mar - riage is the

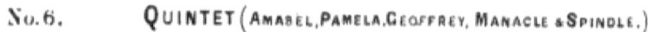

A. sink in - to......... the ground,

P. I...... fore - see.

M. Thus.... do I the bride in -

S. In me... a friend have found,

legg:

A. I...... could sink..... in - to the ground.

P. This is past all jest,.. is really past a jest, And all the blame will

M. - vest...... With the robe, the robe of mys - te - ry.

A. I........ with doubt and fear,.... doubt and

P. blame.... will fall on me,.... yes,... on

M. Cou _ rage then! Cou _ rage then, my

S. Cou _ rage then! Cou _ rage then, my

A. fear! Mar _ riage! at the bare i _

P. me! Mar _ riage! at the bare i _

M. dear, my pret _ ty dear. Mar _ riage is the pa _ na _

S. dear, Cou _ rage!.. Mar _ riage is the pa _ na _

A. _dea.... I could sink in_to the ground. Fill'd am

P. _dea.... We could sink in_to the ground. Fill'd am

M. _ce_a, Our ex_pe_ri_ence has found. Cou_rage

S. _ce_a, Our ex_pe_ri_ence has found. Cou_rage

A. I with doubt and fear!. A_las, if we should here .... be

P. I with doubt and fear! What if we should here .... he

M. then, my pret_ty dear; For in me..... a friend .... you've

S. then, my pret_ty dear; For in... me a friend .... you've

18796.

18796.

M. Restrain'd by cruel te _ _ ther, What fairy spell en _

M. chanting, Their tender wishes granting Shall set them free to _ ge _ ther, to _ ge _

Andante con moto.

M. _ ther? A gold _ en web's be _ fore them,

M. Oh, let them seek.... it's mesh _ es; For those...... who once ex _

M. plore...... them,.... For ev er more.... a _ dore them, Where

M. love..... the soul re _ fresh _ _ es, Where love the soul refresh _ _

A. A gold _ en web's be _ fore them,..

P. A gold _ en web's be _ fore them,..

G. A gold _ en web's be _ fore them,..

M. _ es, A gold _ en web's be _ fore them,..

S. A gold _ en web's be _ fore them,..

18796.

SONG (PAMELA)

I knew a love-song years a-go; . . . . . . Ah, well-a-

-day, . . . 'tis nigh for-got! . . . There were broken hearts in it, I

trow; . . Ah, well-a-day, ... 'tis the common lot! . . .

Ah, well _ a _ day, 'tis the com-mon lot!. There were loves and doves, and moon and June, For 'tis thus that lo-vers make com-mune, 'Tis thus that lo-vers make com-mune. I forget the words, and it had no tune . . . . . . Ah, well-a-day, well-a-day! . . .

18796.

My love-song now is the chink of gold,......

Ah, well-a-day,.... and I've never a jot!.... I love it

more as I grow old,___ Ah, well-a-day,___ and.... what maid does

not?... Ah, well-a-day, and what

maid does not.... For it
rings and sings of a thou _ sand things, Of the joys that
its posses_sion brings, the joys that its pos ses _ sion brings....

poco meno mosso.
Yet that o _ ther song... to my con _ science clings   Ah, well a-

_ day, well-a_day!

a tempo.

colla voce:

18796.

FINALE ACT I.

B. ... Yes, mine's.... the best plan..... Do not hur-ry or har-ry her; Girl....ish ca-price is the prin-ci-pal bar-ri-er... Pa...tience will con-quer it, then.... you can mar-ry her,

S. ... Nay, mine's... the best plan..... I'll be no tar-dy tar-ri-er; If...... you con-sent, to the Fleet I will car-ry her, Wast...ing no time, wil-ly-nil...ly I'll mar-ry her;

18796.

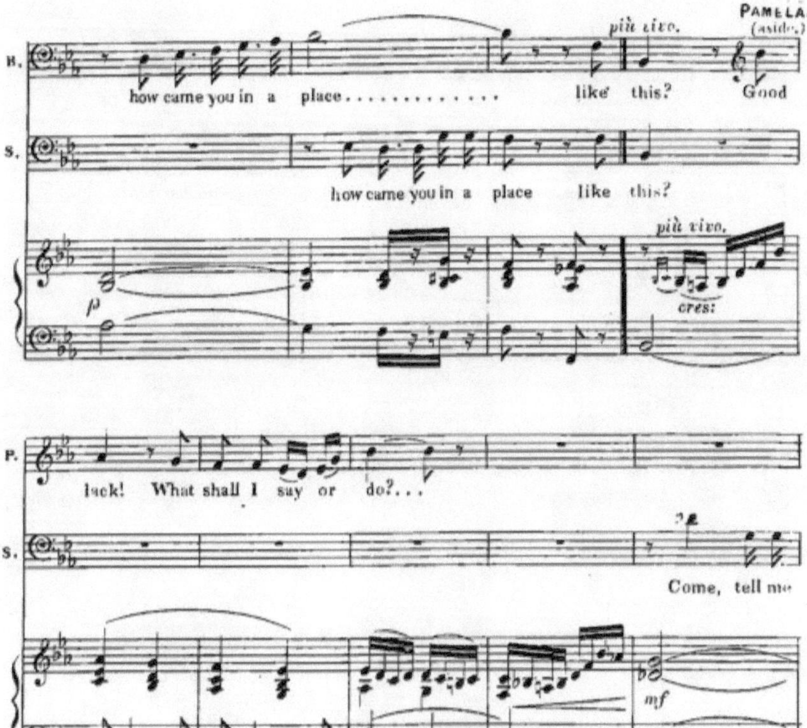
PAMELA. (aside.)
più vivo.
B.
how came you in a place . . . . like this? Good
S.
how came you in a place like this?
p
più vivo.
cres:
P.
lack! What shall I say or do? . . .
S.
Come, tell me
mf
P.
Good lack! what can I say?
S.
all, or you shall rue. A. ha! how well
tr
pp

(aloud)

P. Oh no, in-

S. ... my plan t'would car_ry through If Am _ a _ bel were with her too!

P. _ deed, She is not here! I...... am a_lone,.... as you may

P. see. In_deed, in deed she is not here.

BULL:

S. There's something underhand, I fear. Yes, yes, there's

(hesitating.)

. tend, And,— and know.ing how dis.putes will end, And

feeling prey to wild dis.may! And so I fol.low'd, as I say, And doubtless

doubtless you will comprehend That this is why I'm here to - day, Doubt . . less

(curtsies.)

you will comprehend That this is why I'm here to - day.

BULL.

B. Thy tale is crook— ed as a pig's!

Get home, and run me no more rigs!

Allegro come 1mo. (Bullion goes up to

(Pamela stopping him.)

P. Why, can this be her cloak?

SILVER:

(Manacle's door.)

S. How now?

cres:

P. She's not here now!

BULL:
(knocking.)

S. Is Am . a . bel with . in?

What

cres:

18796.

on - - - ly, 'tis on_ly a question of mo-ney!

ff

'Tis on_ly a question of

ff

'Tis on_ly a question of

ff

poco rit Tempo.

D'ye want to be married, good sirs? D'ye

mo_ney! Ha!

BULL: & SILV: CHOR:

mo_ney! No! no! Ha!

want a nice wife, sweet as ho_ney? The luck....... will be

ha! The luck will be

BULL: & SILV: CHORUS.

ha! No! no! The luck.... will be

me To force my way out of this place. Ho la! ho la!

WOMEN.
luck will be yours and not hers! Ha!

Ha!

Ha!

Come varlets! Come hussies, and aid us! Pray

Ha! D'ye want to be married, good sirs? ..... Here are wenches as plenty as

Ha! D'ye want to be married, good sirs? ..... Here are wenches as plenty as

Ha! D'ye want to be married, good sirs? ..... Here are wenches as plenty as

No, no!.................

sirs! Ha!ha! ha! ha! ha! ha!..................

sirs! Ha!ha! ha! ha! ha! ha!..................

sirs! Ha!ha! ha! ha! ha! ha!..................

(Bullion and Silvertop are hustled into different "marriage shops" by the crowd.)

(Manacle comes out of "The Golden Web" leading Amabel & Geoff: masked. Pamela following.)

Andante con moto.

p

dolce.

115

M. me, E - mo - tion I would bid . . you smo - ther!

rit:

AMABEL.

A. Then tell him he should sink with shame, for yield . ing up his

Allegro moderato:

A. name and fame To one whom he shall nev . . er know!

GEOFF:

G. And tell her that my

G. heart is dead, My love up - on . . . . a false one shed, So

A. And tell him 'tis a shameful

G. free . ly I can bid her go!

A. act That shows a want of heart and tact, And loss of ... self es .

A. . teem!

G. And tell her 'tis not vir . tue moves My heart, as this our

G. part . ing proves,— I .... am not what I seem.

A. Farewell to love,... Fare.well,.... to love for aye!

P. . quit . ed! Farewell to love for aye!

G. . quit . ed! Farewell to love.... for aye for aye!

M. . quit . ed! Farewell to love for aye!

rit:

Andante con moto.

(They go slowly off.)

cres . . . cen . . . do *e* *accelerando.*

poco *a* *poco.*

(The crowd rush out pushing Bullion & Silvertop forward their wigs awry - their clothes torn etc.)

SOP.

CON. Ha! ha! ha! ha! ha! ha! Ha! .....

TENOR. Ha! ha! ha! ha! ha! ha! ....

BASS. Ha! ha! ha! ha! ha! ha! ....

f Allegro come 1mo

(They dance round the old men.)

.... D'ye want to be married, good sirs? .... Here are

D'ye want to be married, good sirs? .... Here are

.... D'ye want to be married, good sirs? ...... Here are

wenches as plenty as fish-es! ...... No aid......... Doc-tor

wenches as plenty as fish-es! ..... No aid.......

wenches as plenty as fish-es! ..... No aid.......

D'ye want to be mar-ried, good

we can ac-complish your wishes! D'ye want to be mar-ried, good

we can ac-complish your wishes! D'ye want to be mar-ried, good

BULL: & SILVER:

No! no! no! no!........ No! no! no! no! no! no!.....

sirs?...... D'ye want a nice wife sweet as honey?.... The luck..... will be

sirs?..... D'ye want a nice wife sweet as honey?.... The luck..... will be

sirs?..... D'ye want a nice wife sweet as honey?... The luck..... will be

18796.

End of Act I

No.9.

ACT II.
CHORUS.

18796.

18796.

18796.

- er a Paradise mor - - - - tals may gain,........ 'Tis here.....

- - - er a Pa - ra - dise..... mor - - tals may gain,.....

ev - er a Pa - ra - dise - mor - - tals may gain,.....

If ever a Pa - ra - dise mor - - tals may gain,.....

... 'tis here!..... 'tis here!

... 'tis here!..... 'tis here!

... 'tis here!..... 'tis here!

... 'tis here!..... 'tis here!

heart of the re — — — — vel-ler filling with rare.....

The heart............. fill — ing with rare.....

The heart............. fill — ing with rare.....

The heart............. fill — ing with rare.....

... de-light,..... rare...... de-light,..... Th-

... de-light,..... rare...... de-light,..... The

... de-light,..... rare...... de-light,..... The

... de-light,..... rare...... de-light,..... The

heart...... of the re _ _ _ vel_ler fill _ _ ing with rare.....

heart of the re _ _ _ vel_ler fill _ ing with rare.....

heart..... of the re _ _ _ vel_ler fill _ ing with rare.....

heart of the re _ _ _ vel_ler fill _ ing with rare.....

... de _ light, with rare...... de_

... de _ light, with rare...... de_

... de _ light, with rare...... de_

... de _ light, with rare...... de_

_light,..... The heart..... of the re_vel_ler fill _ _ _ _

_light,..... The heart of the re _ _ vel_ler fill _

_light,..... The heart.... of the re _ _ _ vel_ler fill _

_light,..... The heart... of the re _ _ _ vel_ler fill _ _

poco rit:

_ing with rare.... de_light!

_ing with rare.... de_light!

_ing with rare.... de_light!

_ing with rare.... de_light!

18796.

No. 10.

BALLET.

18796.

No. 11.

RECIT: (Mrs. Scatterwell, Mrs. Pounceby, Silvertop & Bullion.)

S. time! . . .   Well!

S. well!   I'll   try!   With Beau ty's

S. wish es   all   men   should com ply.

L'istesso tempo.

SCATTER:

Sc. Ah,   yes, with Beauty's wish es, with Beauty's wishes   all men should com

POUN:

P. Ah,   yes, with Beauty's wish es, with Beauty's wishes   all men should com

espress.

Segue Song.

SONG (SILVERTOP) & ENSEMBLE.

S. ho! A maid‒en who, as maidens do, Re‒fus'd his proffer'd suit so

S. true, Tho' he had rank and rich‒es too, So‒ho!.... so‒

Sc. SCATTER: If 'twas So‒ho,

S. risoluto. ‒ho!....with him she would not dwell.

Sc. (They look reprovingly at her) I'm not sur‒pris'd, So whol‒ly she his love des‒pis'd.

18796.

SILV: (with great suavity)

I beg your par_don, I beg your par_don! 'Twas in Hatton Gar_den, in Hutton Gar_den the youth did dwell...

SILV:

He was a knight, as I've heard tell.

SCATTER: (interrupting)

What kind of night? a dark night? short night?

BULLION. (impatiently)

This bids fair to last a

18786.

Sc. says he took her to the Strand; I really can't un—der—stand!

P. Holborn she'd not dwell, in Holborn she'd not dwell.

H. 'Twas in Hat—ton Gar—den they did dwell, I'll bet a

S. best what place it is, Why sing the song your—selves!

Sc. He'll bet a far—den! 'Twas in Hat—ton Garden that they did

P. No! No! 'Twas in Holborn they would not

H. far—den, 'Twas in Hat—ton Gar—den that they did

S. My brain is in a per—fect whizz, in a per—fect whizz, You

far—den, I too will bet a far—den, 'Twas in High Hol—born they did

far—den it was in Hat—ton Gar—den, in Hat—ton Gar—den they did

Since you know best what

den that they........ did dwell!

dwell, that they...... did dwell!

dwell, that they...... did dwell!

place it is, Why sing the song your—selves!

18796.

No.13.

DUET. (PAMELA & SMUG.)

Allegretto Scherzando.

PIANO.

PAMELA.

Don't come near   me!

SMUG.

Deign   to   hear   me—   Let   me

18796.

P. tak _ ing, I con _ fess!

S. On my en _ trea _ ties do... not...

P. Oh, I must let him gent _ ly down! To

S. frown!. . . . . To

P. manners pray give heed! I'm shock'd__ I am in _ deed!

S. manners pray give heed! You're ve _ ry hard in _ deed!

(aloud)

18796.

'Tis best we par _ ted! What

(aside.)

I _ ron heart _ ed!

18796.

man . . ly grace!   How ten . der.

Hope, die! . . . Grief take its place!

. ly he plays his part!

She yields, she yields!   Be

I real ly   am a .

still, my heart!

12796.

P. fraid of you! No! no! well then

S. One lit . tle kiss just one now do!

a tempo.

P. one kiss u . pon my hand! Per .

S. Your hand? no, no, your lips!

(offers her cheek)

P. . haps I'll split the dif . fer . ence with you, And on this

S. Her cheek! O

12796.

SONG (Manacle)

18796.

nets I weave; E'en when in them ly _ ing none my toils per-

_ cieve. Spin on, spin on, weird sis_ters, Shape our mortal line,

Yours the warp and woof, the Golden web.... is mine.

Sel_fish plot ters tremble, vain _ ly

poco rit: dim: a tempo.

have ye wrought... Schemes your hearts dis_sem_ble, schemes that I....

meno mosso.   rit:

meno mosso.   rit:

... can bring to nought,   In _ no_cence and vir_tue on one

colla voce.   a tempo.

friend   a _ lone _ re _ ly,   None shall dis_con_cert you while my

No. 15.

DUET (Amabel & Geoffrey)

Amabel.

Farewell, fare_well! . .

GEOFFREY

O fly me not, my A _ ma_bel! . .

I am not thine!

A _ las! I know it well; but on_ly hear me speak.

_p_ colla voce.

a tempo.

(Looking round.)

Then speedy be; I shall be miss'd and sought for!

A.

G.
e _ ver sun _ _ der me from bliss, ... must ever sunder me from

_ lus! how like our lives and fate! . . . I, . . . too, was bound by sor _ row's
bliss.

_ ter, Time pass'd a _ way, day fol _ low'd day, Yet came no word, no

lov _ ing word or let _ ter. Thou didst renounce me, and with sorrow

rack'd You wreck'd my fu _ _ ture by one fool _ ish act! . . . . . You wreck'd my

18796.

A. never dream'd. For Summer tempests pass away, And while the clouds ob-

A. -scure......... the day, Love,........... in our bosoms sheltereth, And

A. lives........ for aye.

G. Now love is buf_fet_ed with storms, He

A. Ah..... love........ droops his wings.

G. droops his wing, No rain_bow cheers, no sun_light warms...... the

clouds may ne - ver pass a - way, Yet while in grief, in grief our lives de -

clouds may ne - ver pass a - way, Yet while in grief, in grief our lives de -

- cay....... And love.. in our hearts,. in our hearts lies.

- cay....... And love.... in our hearts,. in our hearts lies....

suff'ring, Yet lives for aye........ Love in our hearts;.... lies suff'ring,

suff'ring, Yet lives for aye........ Love in our hearts..... lies suff'ring,

Yet lives for aye!.........

Yet lives for aye!.........

18796.

P. Would you en‿trap me? A‿lack!.. Help!...

S. Come, come!

AMABEL.

P. Ah!... A‿las!............ My aunt!

A. How can the peo‿ple stand and see A dame thus

A. wic‿ked‿ly tre‿pann'd? A‿las!.....

18796.

18796.

GEOFFREY.

G. What do I see? 8va....... My Am...a.bel?

G. To her! Stand back, stand back, you

G. villains!

S. Have a care, have a care, young sir! 8va...... What

G. What right? What right?..... At

S. right have you to in..ter..fere? What right?..

18796.

A.

hence!......................

P.

- pense!

G.

- fence!......

S.

go,...... go from hence!

Yes, let the youth his sword but draw, — 'Tis for his love's de - fence!

Yes, let the youth his sword but draw, — 'Tis for his love's de - fence!

A.

P.

No, no, no, no! In - deed I'm willing, sirs, to go!

G.

Ah false girl!

S.

Ah ha ha ha

Ah ha ha ha

ha! she is not loth to go! Pro _ ceed, proceed,....

ha! she is not loth to go! Pro _ ceed, proceed,....

.... brave wooer, We hail thy daring feat! What tho' the maid be

.... brave wooer, We hail thy daring feat! What tho' the maid be

.... brave wooer, We hail thy daring feat! What tho' the maid be

will _ _ ing, Thy deed... is not less thrill _ ing, Nor thy re_

will _ _ ing, Thy deed... is not less thrill _ ing, Nor thy re_

will _ _ ing, Thy deed... is not less thrill _ ing, Nor thy re_

TENORS.

BASSES.

ward..... less sweet, Nor thy re ward..... less sweet.

ward..... less sweet, Nor thy re ward..... less sweet.

ward..... less sweet, Nor thy re ward..... less sweet.

Dread not our in - ter - fe - rence, Thou a - ged

Dread not our in - ter - fe - rence, Thou a - ged

Dread not our in - ter - fe - rence,

re - probate!

re - probate!

18796.

190

18 796.

A. Ah,...... he loves me still; Yet by

P. Ah hap _ py

G. ...... am I! By cru _ el

S. By cru _ el

ha! ha! ha! ha! ha! ha!...... By cru _ el

ha! ha! ha! ha! ha! ha!

8va

animando.

A. fate from love I'm part _ ed for aye,......

P. day! Oh hap _ py,

G. fate from love I'm part _ ed for aye,......

S. Ah hap _ py day! Oh hap _ py,

fate Two lovers are part _ ed

By cru _ el fate Two lo-vers are part _ ed Two lovers, two lo _ vers are

By cru _ el fate By fate two lo _ vers are

8va animando.

End of Act II.

18796.

ACT III.

CHORUS WITH SOLOS (GEOFFREY & SMUG.)

Allegro moderato.

PIANO.

18796.

18796.

There's e _ nough to drown all care, boys; But re _ mem _ ber,

There's e _ nough to drown all care, boys; But re _ mem _ ber,

pray drink fair, boys,

BASSES.

pray drink fair, boys,

A bottle!

TENORS.

SOPRANOS.

TENORS.

A bot _ tle

Yes a good old bot _ tle! A _

_ maze _ ment, a _ maze _ _ ment and grat _ i _ tude close

BASSES.

A _ maze _ _ ment and grat _ i _ tude close

18796.

up each throt_tle, A glass of such med'_cine out of the

up each throt_tle, A glass out of the

bot_tle Will stir up a blush our com_plexions to mot_tle!

bot_tle Will stir up a blush our com_plexions to mot_tle!

Hurrah! hurrah! for the bottle!

Hurrah! hurrah! for the bottle!

WOMEN.

Now pay!

Now pay!

18796.

please!   Ah, no! then no more li_quor here   will

please!   Ah, no! then no more li_quor here   will

Some o _ ther day!

Some o _ ther day!

flow!   Our mon _ ey please,   Our mon _ ey

flow!   Our mon _ ey please,   Our mon _ ey

Yes, yes, he pays

Sir Geoffrey pays!

cres:

full,   This will make their hearts . . . .   beat quick.

full,   This will make their hearts, their hearts . . . .   beat quick.

Ah, I feel my heart beat quicker. Here's a blessing on the giv.

Ah, I feel my heart beat quicker. Here's a blessing on the giv.

_ er!...

_ er!...

_ er!...

_ er!...

sweet, Yes, sweet,............ sweet is life...........

sweet in the Fleet,........... Life is sweet...........

life is sweet,............ sweet is life...........

life is sweet,........... Life is sweet...........

... in the Fleet!

... in the Fleet!

... in the Fleet!

in the Fleet!

18706.

SMUG.

Allegro.

No more... polite so‿ci‿e‿ty,

PIANO.

f

say,   No more the gen‿tleman

p

play.   I leave my betters to de‿fy   the laws,

p

And get their pun‿ishment   from fe‿male claws.

sfp

18796.

Segue Song.

SONG. (SMUG.)

And down, down, down.... my spirits go To think that she should treat me so,......... To think,.... ...to think that she.... should treat me so! Un__cer__tain are sweet woman's ways, She ne__ver

means the thing she says, She deals in doubt, and loves de . lays, And then she scrat ches when she plays! And down, down, down . . . your spi . rits go To think that she should treat you so, ... To think, . . . to think that she . . . . should treat you so!

S. The more you think your cause is won

S. The more you find it's not be-gun, And

S. when you think, you think you're near the fun, You feel the

S. weight of fif-teen stone!.. Yes, yes, the

S. more you think your cause is won, So much the

SONG (AMABEL)

Love is like a naughty child That none can make o_bey; De_spite the rod, the lit_tle god.... Will al_ways get his way,

This

We coax him here, we drive him there, We threaten and in-veigh,..... He'll pout, he'll pout and cry,... He'll pout,.. he'll pout and cry... but by and bye,.... We find he's got... his way.

This Love is like a

smithy fire,... At first mere ash-es grey,.. You close it in, and

sparks be-gin... From ev'-ry chink to stray. You blow it here,

you rake it there. In vain the bellows play,... Oppos - ing

poco rit: *a tempo.* *poco rit:* *a tempo.*

force........ confirms its course,.... For Love will

colla voce. *a tempo.* *colla voce.* *a tempo.*

have its way, will have its way.

No. 21.

DUET (AMABEL & GEOFFREY)

18798.

10796.

Un _ der the heav'n _ ly dome!...............

Nay, for where love's possess'd.... 'T will glo_ri_fy a prison cell

Nay, for where love's possess'd ... 'T will glo_ri_fy a prison cell

With charms as high..... as cot or dell;

With charms as high, charms as high as cot or

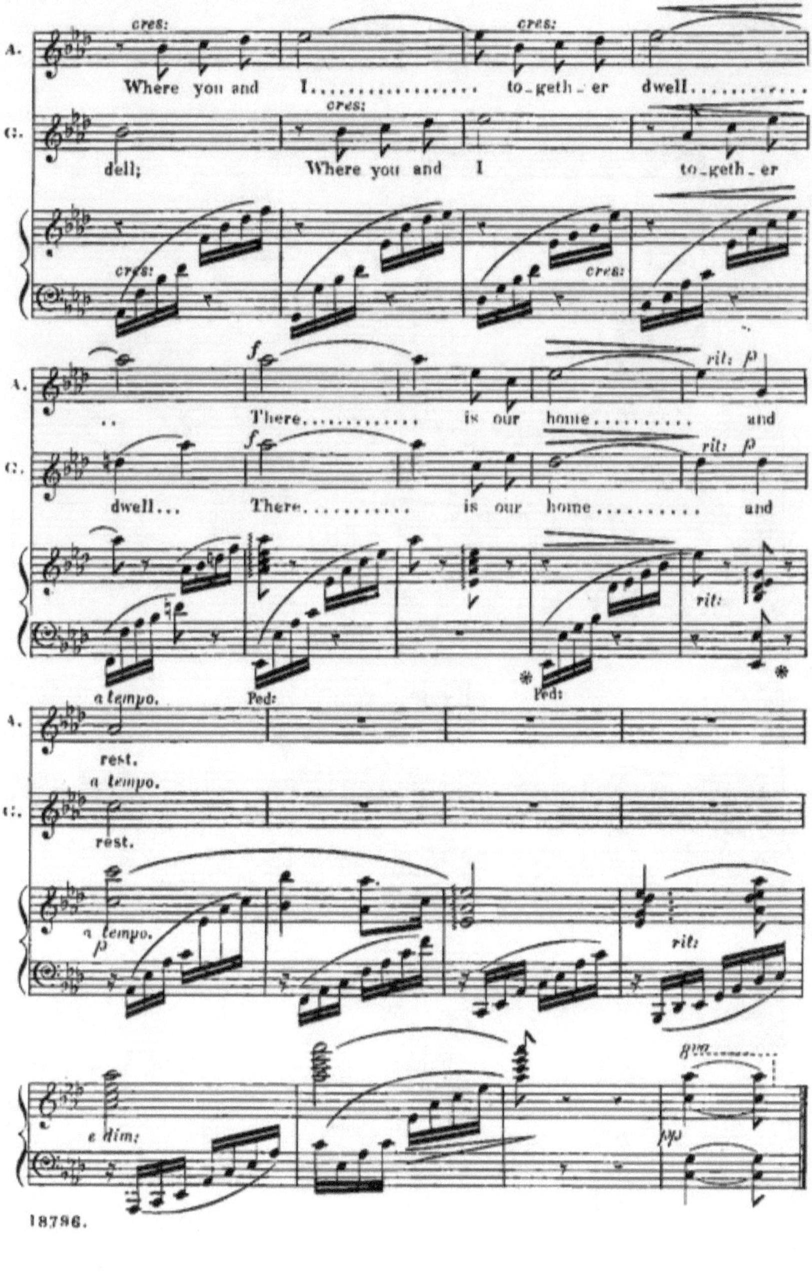
A.
cres:
Where you and I.................. to-geth-er dwell............
G.
dell; cres: Where you and I to-geth-er
cres:
cres:
f
There............ is our home.......... rit: p and
dwell... f There........... is our home.......... rit: p and
rit:
Ped:
Ped:
a tempo.
rest.
a tempo.
rest.
a tempo.
p
rit:
e dim:
8va........
pp

No. 22.

FINALE Act III.

MANACLE.

Yon – der she sits in deep dis – tress! Stand not a – loof............ in this........ her need,...... And let these tears........ for

Tempo di Valse.

M. pi _ _ _ _ ty plead. Re _ mem _ _

M. _ber! Re _ mem _ _ _ ber! she...... is kin to

SULLION (angrily)

M. thee. De _ ceas'd wife's sis _ _ ter is not flesh and

B. blood, And she has dragg'd my ho _ nour

in the mud! Still...... Pa‿me‿la,... I've come...... to pay thy debt. Be this a les‿‿son, a les‿son thou will ne'er...... for‿get.

(advancing towards her)

Tempo.

18796.

MANACLE.

Her heart is full .... She can not

speak — See! .... See ...... how the grate - ful

tears, ... o'er - run .... In par - -

- don - ing this wo - - - man weak

18796.

P. faith _ _ ful lo _ _ ver.

SILV:

B. faith _ _ ful lo _ _ ver. Sweet bride, now let the

M. faith _ _ ful lo _ _ ver.

(He brings forward Pamela who is still disguised in Amabel's Domino)

S. jea _ _ lous mask No more thy fai _ _ ry

PAM:(aside)

P. The plot at last he'll

MAN:

M. Let not the mask thy

BULL:

S. fea _ tures co _ _ ver. Let not the mask thy

18796.

Vivace.

SILVER:

I'm trick'd! I'm swindl'd! I'm trick'd! I'm swindl'd! I've been__ oh!

wed yes, wed To this old wi _ _ _ ther'd

Andante.

AMABEL.
Geor.

Heigh _ ho!

MANACLE.

SILVER:

Gor _ gon's head! Heigh _ ho! Heigh _ ho! The

And so she put him in..... a

maid was old and full of tricks, And so_ And so she put him in..... a

espress.
colla voce.
a tempo.
rit:

18796.

A.

When a mai ‿ den sought your aid you on ‿ ly mock'd.....

P.

When a mai ‿ den sought your aid you on ‿ ly mock'd.....

G.

When a mai ‿ den sought your aid you on ‿ ly mock'd.....

B.
S.

When a mai ‿ den sought your aid you on ‿ ly mock'd.....

A.

.... her! What act of re ‿ pa ‿ ra ‿ tion can be an ‿ y

P.

.... her! What act of re ‿ pa ‿ ra ‿ tion can be an ‿ y

G.

.... her! What act of re ‿ pa ‿ ra ‿ tion can be an ‿ y

B.
S.

.... her! What act of re ‿ pa ‿ ra ‿ tion can be an ‿ y

'Tis sure your own! If an_y plot_ted here for

e _ vil ends T'was you my friends! When all is

cres:

known you must con _ fess with shame I'm not to

blame! Young people, see the end of my de _ signs_

meno mosso.

colla voce.

AMABEL, col soprani.
PAMELA, col contralti.
GEOFFRY, con tenori.
SILVERTOP,
MANACLE, — with basses.
BULLION,

End of Opera.

www.ingramcontent.com/pod-product-compliance
Lightning Source LLC
Chambersburg PA
CBHW030800020726
47499CB00006B/1699